This book
belongs to:

- - - - - - - - - - - -

Two Naughty Piglets

BRIMAX

Two Naughty Piglets

Polly and Percy Piglets live
on Yellow Barn Farm.

They don't mean to be naughty–
but somehow, they always are!

Today they are very excited
because Farmer Jones has
a new red tractor.

"Shall we see if Farmer Jones will give us a ride in his tractor?" snorts Percy.

The two little piglets trot into the farmyard.

There is the red tractor – all new and shiny.

But Farmer Jones is nowhere to be seen!

The two naughty piglets know that they should wait for Farmer Jones, but Percy is too excited.

"Let's sit inside," he says to Polly, and he jumps up into the tractor.

"This is great," Percy shouts.

Polly is too short to climb up.

"Please help me," she squeaks, standing on tiptoe.

Percy leans down and pulls Polly up into the tractor, but he slips!

The naughty piglets tumble down inside the tractor.

Somehow, they undo the brake!

The tractor begins to move.
It rolls across the farmyard.

"Help!" squeaks Polly.

"Help!" squeals Percy.

"Help!" squawk the hens, flapping
all over the farmyard.

Feathers fly everywhere as turkeys
and cockerels flap out of the way!

The tractor rolls into the barn
and crashes into the hay.

The barn is in a terrible
mess when the tractor stops.

Farmer Jones rushes into the barn and sees all the mess.

"You naughty little piglets!" shouts Farmer Jones. "No mud baths for a whole week."

"We're very, very sorry!" say Polly and Percy, shaking. They are very scared.

The naughty piglets scamper away as fast as their legs can carry them.

Polly and Percy go to their sty and lie down in the hay.

"From now on, we will always try to be good little piglets," they grunt.

Here are some words in the story. Can you read them?

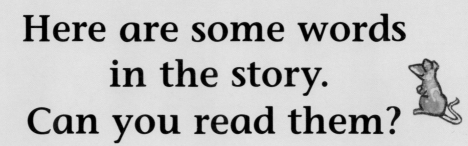

farm	hens
piglet	turkey
farmer	cockerels
red tractor	barn
jump	hay
feathers	sty

How much of the story can you remember?

What is new at Yellow Barn Farm?

Who jumps into the tractor first?

What does the tractor do?

Where does the tractor stop?

What does Farmer Jones say to the piglets?

What do the piglets promise to do?

Can you match the pictures to make four pairs?

Notes for parents

The Yellow Barn Farm stories will help to expand your child's vocabulary and reading skills.

Key words are listed in each of the books and are repeated several times - point them out along with the corresponding illustrations as you read the story. The following ideas for discussion will expand on the things your child has read and learnt about on the farm, and will make the experience of reading more pleasurable.

• Ask your child to point out the naughty piglets in each of the illustrations, and make the animal noises together.

• Talk about all the other animals in the story, the noises they make, where they sleep, and what they eat.

• Talk about all the different machinery used on a farm, for example tractors and ploughs, and what these machines do.

• If possible relate the animals and objects seen in Yellow Barn Farm to real animals and objects in your child's daily life. Point them out to your child so they can bridge the gap between books and reality, which will help to make books all the more real!